SLAVE

SLAVE

RICHARD ALPHONSO TULLOCH

ISBN-13:
ISBN-10:
Library of Congress Control Number:

1

I T IS DARK here, where I sit. Darkness surrounds me, but I am not a broken man, for I am in chains. I know of my existence, yet I have not seen my own face.

Many moons ago, I knew how it felt to have life—a family, a wife—but it was all taken from me.

I am in chains, but I am not a broken man, for I am a slave.

Slavery indulges my body, my soul, but my will is strong. This is what I see. In my mind, there is no turning back. I do not remember how long it has been since I was taken, but I have accepted death; Then freedom, these are my options.

The key turns, forcing the bolt to move. I can hear the metal rumbling as the giant door gets pushed open. Squeaking and crying, light suddenly consumes the darkness covering in the mist. I cannot see, for I am now blinded by the light, but I hear two giant steps coming toward me.

"Get up."

I am a slave, so I will obey. Kneeling on my right knee, my mind tells my body to obey.

"Get up, slave."

I am still chained. Chains hold me to the wall, my body bent forward, unable to stand straight. I can feel the heat from the sun peeking through the door around his massive being as if trying to reach the light that shines bright from my heart. Sweat rolls down my back, but I feel the warm light breeze accompanied by the aroma of pure hatred he holds for me.

"Get up," he repeats, but I cannot get up, for I am a slave, and I am chained.

He knows this. He stands directly behind and above me. I can sense the whispering of his beating heart, smell the stench from his body, and hear the unwilling desire for goodness from each deep breath he takes. A fiddling sound? He starts to raffle back and forth, but I cannot see, for I am a slave, and I am chained.

What is he doing?

He steps forward twice, then once again. Suddenly, it is as if a tiger has sunk its claws in my back and started ripping away. My body does not get a chance to speak to my mind. Everything seems normal, only the pain was slow. Another! My back arches forward. I fall to my knees. My head rises up to the dark, cold roof, as I let out a hoarse scream from the vicious pain.

"Slave, get up."

He is no longer whispering. Sunlight fades in and out. I can only see his shadow on the wall before me. Everything has slowed down. The pain and I are now one. It all becomes clear when his whip slices across my back, reaching all the way around to my belly. I have felt this pain before, but there is no getting used to it. I can only bear it. I scream even harder after the third strike. Looking up, I now see my own blood on the walls around me. The fourth strike, then the fifth, followed by the sixth . . . I scream, but nothing came out. My head arches all the way back, on both knees. Unconsciously, I pull on the chains holding my arms, my body, and all of me, causing me to fall on my back.

"Get up, slave."

I am not a broken man, for I am no longer in chains, but I am still a slave, so I will obey. Puddles of my own blood cover the ground. I slowly turn around, now facing him as I rise to my feet. I look but cannot see his face. Blocked by the sun, his warm breath appears as he speaks.

"Good, slave. Good."

2

I T IS BRIGHT here where I stand. We all stand together, but I am still alone. It is hot. It is bright. The sun stares directly down on me, but I cannot see. I force my eyes open. I can feel the heat chewing away at my flesh. Sweat rolls down my back and stings my fresh wounds. I can hear the vultures circling above. They can sense, just like I do, that we are all rotten carcasses, and they wait. My body trembles. Pain consumes me, but I stand here beneath the sun, for I am no longer chained, but I am still a slave. My mind remains strong, I know this.

Wait! Someone approaches. There are no sounds but the footsteps. I do not move or make a sound. Someone appears in front of me. A shadow? I still have not seen the face of the man who pulled me from my dungeon. Squinting, I see . . . a woman? She faces me. Her head blocks the sunlight, and her hair! Yes, her hair blows with the hot, moist breeze. I see her face. She is beautiful. Clearly, she is not a slave. But I am! I am a slave. I am no longer chained, but I am a slave. She pores water over my head. It burns, but a cool sensation flows over my body. I see pity in her eyes, perhaps for me, or maybe it is the reflection of what she sees. It was not just me. We stand here, men, slaves, rounded up like live stocks.

"Slaves, move forward."

We move as one, following the person in front. It is unknown to me where we are going, but it does not matter, because I am no longer chained, but I am still a slave. I can feel the hot desert sand chewing away at the sole of my feet. I do not know how long I have been walking, but one step after another, I continue forward. Look back I will not, as I still see vultures circling above, just waiting to feast on our dead flesh. I no longer feel sweat running down my body, just pain. So thirsty. I need water.

"Slaves, stop."

I recognize that voice as the man who pulled me from my dungeon. We all immediately stand still, our back arched, body and mind trembling. I slowly pull my dry lips apart, pain rushing down my throat as I try to swallow. The sun stands directly over me, searing the wounds on my back. Tilting my head sideways, I see something. A mirage, perhaps? It must be. The Gods must be mocking me. I see . . . mountains, mountains that touch the heavens.

"Look!"

Someone shouts. I turn my head, realizing I was not the only one. We all stand staring in the same direction, so perhaps it is not a mirage.

"Slaves. . . ."

It is the man who pulled me from my dungeon, I cannot see him, but I am certain. That voice brings darkness to the light and pain to my body. I hear the hatred that consumes it. He speaks.

"Slaves. Today is a day of righteousness, a day of revolution. For you, at least . . . Ha ha ha ha . . .

"Today is a day for hope and faith. But, unfortunately, because you are all slaves, it can also be a day for despair, pain, agony, and even death. Let it be known that most of you will die today.

"Hell, ha ha ha ha, maybe even all of you. But freedom is just a whisper away. Look before you. What you see is what you want to see. After I am done speaking, you will no longer be slaves.

Why? Why, you ask? Today, you will all be freed . . . well, at least released from slavery, that is.

"What does this mean? It means you run . . . Run, because you no longer need to obey. But be aware, slaves, of that first step. The second you start running, you become our prey, and you will be hunted down like dirty dogs.

"If you are caught, death will come only after I pull your heart from your stinking chest. This is the absolute. If you decide not to run, you will be given a swift and sudden death right where you stand. But if you can overcome your fear and your weakness and make it to the top of those mountains standing before you, your life will be spared, and you will be free to roam this filthy world as a man.

"So run, I say! For you are not to be hunted as slaves. You will be hunted as men. Do not look back. Remember, whether it is freedom or death, from this point, you are no longer a slave. You are free. So, run. Run! Ha ha ha ha."

3

I T IS GETTING dark here as I run. I hear screams behind me, but I dare not to look. A chance at freedom has numbed all the pain in my body. My feet feel strong. I feel my toes dig away at the hot sand as I run. I am not running alone—I see shadows all around me—but we do not run as one. I can still hear the screams behind me from the men too afraid to run. No, not me. I will run, for I am not chained, and I am no longer a slave, so I will run. My eyes are locked toward freedom, toward those tall mountains ahead. I feel strong. Mind, body, and soul are all prepared for this. If I could just at least make it to the tree line, I might have a chance. A difficult task that brings me absolute freedom, so I will try . . . for I am not chained, and I am no longer a slave. Death first, then freedom; those are my only options. It is getting dark, but for the first time, it has never been so bright. Shadows of men scattered in the dessert all running in the same direction, for the same purpose.

I first feel the impact. Then I feel my face sliding along the hot sand. I was now lying face first in the dessert spitting out sand. I fell? How? No, I must get up. My mind wonders, but my body stays on path. I roll over, spitting sand from my mouth. No! Wait! What is this? A body lies directly in front of me. He was not moving. Pain suddenly reenters my body. Now I see it. It is everywhere. Death! I am surrounded by nothing but death. Free men who were once slaves . . . This is what caused me to fall. I stare at him. He had died, and I tripped over his body. The arrow protruding from his head gave it away. Even though the sun was no longer directly above, vultures still circled, waiting to feed on dead. It became clear. Prey. That is what I am. I am not chained, and I am no longer a slave, but I am being hunted. Footsteps? They are coming to take my life. I see them in the distance. Death.

I am sitting in the desert sand, looking in the wrong direction. Death is what I see. His head turns all the way back, body thrashes forward, and arms lock to the side. Blood squirts from his neck as his body slams in the sand. He is dead before the sword is pulled from his neck. Blood fills the sand as I watch another man, once a slave, running for freedom, but the sword from a man behind him swiftly penetrates his back. He falls to his knees, but he is still alive. He is not too far from me. He looks down, then up at me. A thick layer of blood pours from his mouth. I see it in his eyes. It is the same look I saw in the woman's eyes earlier. It is not fear or pity, just a reflection of what he sees. I must get up. I must run. One after the other, I see my feet digging in the sand. My thighs burn, as I run in the direction of the mountains. Dead bodies surround me, with the brown sand being soaked in red blood. Only a few of us remain running

in the same direction. Death has somehow consumed every-
one else. I can hear them behind us, screaming and yelling,
but I dare not to look back. The tree line is just up ahead,
not too far.

Again, it is if I am struck by lightning. The force knocks
me to the ground. I scream as I feel the impact. This is an
unfamiliar pain stretching from my right shoulder all the way
down my back. I reach over with my left arm to feel the tip of
an arrow. It had passed straight through my back all the way
to my chest. No, no . . . They are trying to kill me. I am on
my knees, pushing my body off the ground, I must get up.
Footsteps? They keep coming closer to me, and they are not
of a man but a horse. Raising my body and facing up, I see a
man on a horse riding toward me. They are all on horses, but
only one rides toward me. It is not clear to see, but I can feel
the warm stream of blood running down my chest. It was
clear that he was sent to bring death upon me while the others
watch in the distance.

Cowards!

Only a short distance away, he stops and slides down the
side of his horse. His feet hit the sand. With haste, he walks
toward me. I can smell the filthy aroma of dark hatred he has
for me and taste of his sweet, unconditional desire to kill. They
all stand calm on their horses further in the distance, watching,
waiting for him to rip my life from my body. He unsheathes his
sword. I am not chained and no longer a slave, but just a few
more steps and death will be upon me. There is no hesitation
in his body as he raises the sword over his head.

Screams. Screams fill the desert. His head rises to the sky as he screams. He screams so loud, it provokes God's thunder. His sword falls from his hand, as he drops to his knees.

I had somehow plucked the arrow from my chest and unkindly buried it in his heart.

His body falls over me as I continue to push deeper. Warm blood comes pouring out onto my face. I look into his eyes, but I see not what I saw in the woman's earlier. It was fear, fear of death that I have brought on him. Death is what I see. It is soon clear to the men on the horses what I have done.

I am still alive.

I scream . . . in the wrong direction. They slowly start riding toward me as if waiting for me to run. This is so they can start their chase. The predators hunger their prey.

Sword.

I grab the sword and turn toward the mountains. I was not too far from the trees, now. Whatever strength I have left, I will use to run in the right direction, away from the predators and toward those trees. I have made it!

Looking back, they all stand with their horses next to the body of the boy I had stabbed the life out of. They are three, but only one gets off his horse. He is looking directly at me. The daylight is gone. I am not chained and no longer a slave. I make it to the tree lines but as a prey, this is for certain. I am being hunted down, and they want to bring death upon me.

4

THE SKY WAS dark now as I run. Lightning continuously strikes, and thunder roars like a lion from above. I can feel the anger from the Gods as the clouds explode in the night sky. I feel each single drop of rain on my skin. The cold drops of water seep into my wounds. My toes dig across the mud. Both legs push me forward. My hands grab the trees, limbs, barks, pulling my body forward and upward. I will not stop tonight. I must try to get ahead. I am not chained and no longer a slave, but I am a prey. They are hunting me. My body has dissolved into this darkness, and I no longer know me. For a long time, I have not seen myself. The Gods have cursed me, but today, I choose to live. I now feel life running through my veins. I am alive, not as a slave and not chained.

I have traveled very far through the forest as I look from where I had run. Where I stand, I stand over the world. The forest slopes downward, so I can see over the trees. Looking in the direction I had just come from, I see where the forest ends and where the desert begins. The rain has suddenly stopped. Droplets of water roll down and drip from the leaves and onto my face. It is quiet, except for the howling wind sweeping through the forest. Droplets of rainwater fall into puddles on the ground. The night has been long, for the sun is now rising. I embrace the energy the warmth brought to me. Now I realize where I stand. My eyes look to the skies. My mind opens to the surroundings.

Dead rotting corpses surround me. The stench becomes stronger as my mind and eyes become clearer. Fresh carcasses, bloody bones, lifeless bodies filled with maggots . . . A reflection of what they saw just before life was pulled from their bodies . . . Death, everywhere.

But it is not the stench the dead that fills my nose. It was pure, vicious sight of their remains that will surely follow me to the afterlife. I turn to run toward freedom. The mountain is very steep, and there was nowhere to go but up. Death first, then freedom. These are my only options.

So, I will climb.

Straight up is the only place to look as I climb up the rocky mountain. As I climb higher, everything grows dark, black like burnt out coal, and it has started to cover my hands, feet, and my whole body. I climb. I feel the rocks rip away at my hands, piercing through the skin on my palms. I grab on to the rocks tightly to prevent me from falling. The mountain is still wet, and the rocks are slippery. My body is now fully covered in black from this mountain, but I care not. I care only about climbing and making it to the top, making it to freedom. I know not if I am closer to the top. I can only see glimpse of the sunrays, for I am now between two mountains.

My body is fully covered in black soot. My clothes are completely rippled and covered in blood. As I reach over to gain leverage, I realize how extremely high up I now am. If I were to fall, it would surely be my demise, but I care not. Now, as I pull my body up, my mind is not really sure what it is seeing. There is a small ledge I am able to climb up on. Standing upright, looking up between two mountains, the cloudy skies seem even darker.

It is now raining again. The two mountains are now closer to each other. Yes, I know I can see something. I see a man. He clearly stands above and across from where I am. Looking down at me, it is as if I were looking in the mirror. His skin is fully covered in black soot. His body and clothes are red with blood. Even though it is raining, the blood stains his body. We both stand straight up, staring at each other. Lightning, thunder, and rain poured down our bodies. I am not a slave, for I am not chained. It is obvious that the only way to the top of this mountain is through him.

5

I STAND STARING AT this man. Who is he?
Rain drips from his body, and blood stains on his face. Though we are not close to each other, it was as if we can see into each other's eyes. It is now or never, so I start to climb. As I continue, the space between two mountains grows smaller. I can now jump across. The man stands for a second, watching as I advance. I climb onto another ledge and continue to stare at him. He then takes two steps back, then a third out of sight. It is now pouring. Thunder and lightning fill the skies. Suddenly, a sensation fills me. I know not what this strange feeling is, but it is not familiar. A thick, black liquid substance fills the skies above as I look up. I stare and watch as it seems to fill the air above me. Confusion fills my mind, as I stand still, staring. It consumes me, engulfing my entire body. It is instant—the pain—for it is boiling tar. I let go and fall face first onto the ledge. Pain like no other consume my mind, body, soul, spirit, and all that I am. I know I am screaming, but I do not hear a sound, for all my senses are listening to the burning pain radiating from my body. I am bent over,

kneeling, palms down. I now smell burning flesh. Where I stand is now engulfed in flames. I am being burnt alive. At this instant, I stand in the middle of a fiery, blazing, burning tar, and the flames stand above me, for I am on my knees. Freedom first, then death. Those are my options. The flames are high, and I am surrounded by them, but still I am able to stand. I know if I do not find a way to get away from where I am, my burnt body would be feeding the vultures in the morning. So I jump! I jump, knowing I can reach across to the other mountain. I just need to grab onto whatever I can. I kept reaching and reaching, and nothing. There is nothing for me to hold onto. My body is still on fire, flying across the rainy breeze. Straight through my right chest, I feel the piercing of an arrow. Blood pours from my mouth. I fall forward on a ledge. One hand reaches for the thundering skies, the other holds on to the arrow that has pierced through the right side of my chest. From a glimpse, I notice it was the man on the other side of the mountain. He takes aim again with his bow and arrow. This arrow has a flaming tip, and it is aimed directly at me. He releases it, and I watch it go straight through my lower abdomen. This time, all my senses allow me to scream. I am not a slave, and I am no longer chained.

With both arrows still in my body, and my skin still completely burnt, I immediately start to climb. I can smell my burning flesh as I pull my half-dead body up this mountain. I can now see his expressions clearly. I can tell he is wondering how I am still alive. Tears roll down my cheeks as I pull my body up rock by rock, ledge by ledge.

Again, a large, black substance completely covers the sky. This time, it is solid and round. It is loud, louder than the thunders. Is it rolling? It is! It is rolling down to take my life. It is an extremely large boulder. It is so large that it keeps bouncing back and forth between the two mountains. He had pushed it, and it is now rolling toward me, crashing and breaking off parts of the mountain, and it is coming to kill me. Just a few feet above me, I see a small area to escape, and I jump. The boulder rolls down the side of the mountain, just ripping the burning skin from my back as it passes. The pain shoots through my body. I lie down belly first. I do not know if I can get up. As I push my hands, knees, and toes in the mud beneath me, I am able to rise. Now, I am close to him. I pull myself up and over the final ledge. I am finally at the top. The man stands in front of me. Glaze covers my eyes. Yet, I am standing. I look straight at him, and he stares at me. My first step is in a deep puddle of rainwater. He does not move. On my second step, I notice both the arrows are still protruding from my body. He does not move. My third step, I do not remember.

"Warrior, get up."

He is still standing. The sunlight slowly fades in. His shadow on the side of the mountain vanishes before me.

"Get up, warrior."

That voice. A familiar voice. I am not a broken man, for I am no longer in chains, and I am not a slave. Puddles of my own blood cover the ground. I look at him and now I can clearly see his face. His warm breath appears as he speaks, "Get up, warrior. Freedom awaits."

I stand on one knee, then on two. Pushing my body up, my eyes follow, as I now stand before him, looking straight into his eyes.

"Stand, warrior, for you are free."

His eyes are very familiar. He still stands before me. This familiar voice . . . the man back at the dungeon. But what I see in his eyes is not hatred. What I see in his eyes is . . . not hate, for he is my father.